Telephone
of the
Tree

Telephone
of the
Tree

Alison McGhee

Rocky Pond Books

ROCKY POND BOOKS
An imprint of Penguin Random House LLC, New York

First published in the United States of America by Rocky Pond Books,
an imprint of Penguin Random House LLC, 2024

Text copyright © 2024 by Alison McGhee
Illustrations copyright © 2024 by Danah Kim

Visit us online at PenguinRandomHouse.com.

Library of Congress Cataloging-in-Publication Data is available.

Printed in the United States of America

ISBN 9780593698457
ISBN 9780593857151 (INTERNATIONAL EDITION)

1st Printing

LSCC

Design by Cerise Steel
Text set in Amasis MT Pro

To Birgitt Kollmann, dear friend,
magician translator, she who has long divined
the heart and soul of my books, with love

How I picture the night Kiri and I first met each other, first looked into each other's eyes, first reached for each other's hand, back when we were babies:

The moon like a bright white ship sailing through the sky.

Tree limbs dark against the moonlight, branches reaching to the invisible sun.

Kiri's mom holding Kiri tight in her arms and dancing Kiri down the block.

My dad holding me tight in his arms and dancing me down the block.

In the bright moonlight they dance their crying babies up and down the block so we'll stop crying, so we'll be peaceful, so we'll . . .

sleep

sleep

sleeeeeeep

I picture Kiri's mom and my dad whispering the names
of all the trees to Kiri and me as they dance us past:

oak maple willow

birch pine mulberry

crabapple ginkgo butternut

and all those whispers weave their way into our hearts
that night, so that night of dancing with the trees becomes
the night that made

Kiri and me

love trees

maybe even

want to *be* trees

because of their tall, strong calm

Almost all the trees on our block were planted to celebrate new babies—

oak for Pops
maple for Dad
mulberry for Mrs. S
weeping willows for Rowan and Geneva
little crabapple for Gentleman
baby birch for me
baby pine for Kiri

The oak and maple and mulberry trees are tall and wide now. They've been growing as long as Pops and Dad and Mrs. S have been alive.

But two of the trees were planted not for new babies, but in remembrance of people who passed on.

The ginkgo in honor of Mrs. S's husband, Douglas, because he loved their beautiful fan-shaped leaves.

The butternut in honor of my grandmother Randa, because she loved to eat butternuts.

Fast-forward to second grade. Kiri and I are in Mr. Nesbitt's class. He has just told us all to draw a *What Do You Want to Be?* picture.

"Imagine yourselves at age thirty," he says.

Thirty?

Kiri and I are seven. It takes a long time for us just to count to thirty. We look at each other.

"I mean, my *mom* is thirty," Kiri whispers.

"My parents are thirty-*one*," I whisper back.

Will we ever be that old? When we get to that age, will we *feel* old?

Thirty is so, so far in the future.

But Kiri and I know what we want to be. We've always known, known from the night our parents danced us past the trees.

I look over at Kiri, who's already drawing, sketching an outline on rough paper.

Tall brown trunk. Branches curving downward, filled with pine cones. A child with braids and a round face smiling out of the trunk itself.

"White pine!" I say.

Kiri nods and smiles. Their own white pine, planted in front of their house at the end of the block when Kiri was born, is already taller than they are.

My turn.

I pick up a tan crayon and a white crayon and a green crayon and begin to draw.

White trunks split at the base and curve upward. Papery branches float out and up. Green leaves dance on limbs.

"River birch!" Kiri says.

"Yup!"

Then:

"*TREES?*" Martina says in her Martina voice. "Kids can't be *TREES*."

Martina always, somehow, knows what to say to make others feel bad.

Right away my hand covers up the drawing. Right away Martina's eyes flash and she smirks. She knows she's gotten to me.

Martina always gets to me.

But not to Kiri.

"What's your problem, Martina?"

Kiri is calm, and their voice is soft, and their question *sounds* like a question but isn't. What Kiri is really saying is *back off.*

"Mr. Nesbitt told us to draw what we *want* to be, right?" Kiri continues. "And Ayla and I want to be trees."

Kiri has power.

Kiri has *presence.*

Kiri is already like a tree.

"Ayla and I are dreaming big," Kiri says to Martina. "Why shouldn't we?"

Yeah, why shouldn't we? I think, and we look at Martina until she frowns and backs away.

Kiri makes everything better.

That day in Mr. Nesbitt's class is the day I learn you don't have to make up an excuse for what you want to be.

You can just dream big.

Kiri and I are ten now. Second grade was a long time ago, but we still dream big.

I still think about that day, though. I see Martina's face and the way she backed slowly away from our table, as if there were a force field around it.

I see Mr. Nesbitt's head, bent over his desk. His dark hair fallen across his face, and his pencil scribbling *shhh-shhh-shhh* across the same rough paper the rest of us used back then.

I wish Kiri were around right now. It's easier to dream big when they're with me.

Junie For Short must wish Kiri were here too. Junie For Short is Kiri's dog, and sometimes these days she just howls and howls.

"Junie sure misses Kiri," my mom says. "Just like the rest of us."

"Her name is Junie For Short," I say. "Don't call her Junie."

Junie For Short's real name is Juniper, but that name was too big for the tiny puppy she used to be. So Kiri and I nicknamed her Junie, for short, only what stuck was the whole thing: Junie For Short.

I don't howl, but *I* miss Kiri too.

I picture Kiri, calm and strong, like a tree.

Kiri, come home.

Just as I'm thinking that, Junie For Short, all the way down the block at Kiri's house, begins to howl again, as if she can hear my thoughts.

"That dog's always crying these days," says a voice from the sidewalk.

"I bet she misses Kiri," says a child's voice, and at the sound of those voices I stay

still

still

still

in my birch tree, because I know the voices are Gentleman and his mother. Gentleman is a nickname too. His real name is Fraser, but no one calls him that except his parents, and only when they're angry with him.

Which is a lot.

Not today, though.

Since Kiri left, I try to avoid Gentleman, but it's kind of impossible because he lives on our block.

He keeps asking me about Kiri, like he's worried or something, like he wants me to talk. Like he doesn't like me being quiet.

He tells me to call Kiri.

"I can't," I tell him. "There's no phone where Kiri is."

"Text them, then."

"Gentleman. You need a phone to text."

"Well then, go visit!"

I just close my eyes and shake my head. There's a lot that Gentleman doesn't understand, about phones and a whole lot else. So as he and his mom pass by my tree, I shrink up against it, hoping he won't see me.

It's futile. Up he comes to me in my tree. Five years old and full of swagger. The top of his head, with its sproingy wild curls, bobs in my direction.

You can't deny it, Gentleman's a cute kid.

But he's also a pain, with his constant chatter. His constant *But why are you so quiet these days* and *Why don't you just call Kiri*.

"Go home, Gentleman," I say. "Your mom's going to start yelling for you any second."

Through the birch leaves I see his mom's almost at their apartment building. *Hey! Come back and get your kid,* I think.

But then I see that Gentleman doesn't look like his usual self. His eyes aren't bright, the way they usually are. He just looks at me.

Then: "Can I tell you something, Ayla?"

I shrug. It's no use to say no. If Kiri were here, we'd give each other a secret *here he goes again* look.

He looks at me with those un-bright, un-Gentleman eyes.

"Ayla," he whispers. "Sweetheart died."

"Oh no! Sweetheart, your gecko?"

He nods. Leans against a low limb of my birch tree. His mouth is pressed tight in a way that looks the way my own mouth suddenly feels, which is a *don't cry* sort of feeling.

Those eyes of his. So sad.

This is terrible.

The idea of Sweetheart being dead is too hard to handle. Gentleman loves that lizard as much as Kiri loves Junie For Short.

"How did Sweetheart die?" I ask.

"My mom says 'How should I know, I'm not a vet,'" he says. "My dad says I probably fed her something bad for her."

"Like what?"

"Like a Cheerio," he whispers. "Sometimes. For a treat."

It doesn't seem as if a Cheerio once in a while would kill a gecko. And it seems like a mean thing to say to a little tiny kid who just lost their best lizard friend. But Gentleman's parents aren't like mine.

"Now I know why Junie For Short keeps howling," he says. "It's because she misses—"

Suddenly Gentleman's voice gets quieter and quieter and I can't hear what he's saying.

Or maybe his voice doesn't get quieter. Maybe I can't hear him because I shut my ears down.

If you think

lalala or *nonono*

LOUD

inside your own mind . . .

LALALA

it drowns out everything in the outside world.

Remember this. It's a useful skill when someone says something you don't want to hear.

LALALA

I chant inside my head the whole time Gentleman leans against my birch limb talking about whatever he's talking about, maybe Sweetheart or maybe Junie For Short and her howling or maybe—

LALALA

Finally, Gentleman stops talking, which is good because if you have to *lalala* for a long time, you get tired.

"So now you know the whole story," he says. "Thanks for listening, Ayla."

I don't know the whole story. I don't know any of the story, actually, because of the *lalala,* but I nod anyway. It would be mean not to.

Until Kiri gets home it's up to me alone to take care of the trees on our block. We're the keepers of the trees. If you spend enough time around trees, you learn what they need.

And Kiri and I spend more time in and around the trees on our block than anyone.

"Ayla! Kiri! You're treeing again!"

That's what Kiri's mom says, laughing most of the time, when she finds us climbing up Mrs. S's mulberry tree, or hiding in one of Geneva's and Rowan's weeping willows.

Once my dad said that if we could, we'd *live* in our trees.

He's not wrong.

I mean, wouldn't you want to live in a tree if you could?

If it hasn't rained for a while, Kiri and I water the trees on the block. We fill our buckets halfway from the hose at my house and then carry the buckets to each tree in turn.

back and forth

hose to bucket to tree

sloooooooowly

watering their roots

Even big trees need water. That's something a lot of people don't know, but it's true. You're never big enough not to need water.

Some tree scientists believe trees help each other when one's in need. That they even talk to each other underground, through the fungi that travel along their roots.

Kind of like me and Kiri.

We spend so much time with each other, we can feel what each other needs.

Which is why I want them to come home. It's like I'm missing part of myself. Part of my own root system.

I can't think about it too much or my thoughts get dizzy and swirl around the way Rowan's and Geneva's weeping willow branches dip and toss when a storm is coming.

Tonight, my mom comes upstairs to tuck me in, the way she or my dad always does. I tell her about Gentleman and Sweetheart, his gecko. I tell her how sad Gentleman looked.

I don't tell her about the *lalala*.

Or Junie For Short and her howling.

She smiles and taps her fingertips up and down my arm in a slow rhythm, the way she's done all my life at bedtime. My dad comes in just as I'm telling her my birch tree is thirsty, and that tomorrow I'll drag the hose over to it.

"You've been the keeper of the trees since you were born, daughter," he says in his quiet voice.

You hardly ever hear my dad's voice, but you know he's listening because his eyes, so brown, never leave yours.

He listens and listens and listens.

My parents are not like Gentleman's parents. Have they ever yelled at me? Once or twice, maybe.

"Me and *Kiri* are the keepers of the trees," I correct my dad.

Not just our trees, either. All the trees on the block, the trees planted when each of us was born, the burr oak and maple and weeping willows and crabapple and mulberry.

And the remembrance trees too, the ginkgo and the butternut.

My mom and dad turn off the light and shut my door when they leave, the way they always do.

But when they're downstairs I sneak over and open the door a little. Just a tiny bit, so I can hear the sound of them downstairs.

Sometimes at night now I *lalala* so I won't think about Kiri being so far away.

Or Kiri's mom, who isn't far away, who's just down in their house at the end of the block, and of Junie For Short, who's there with her, but who I also don't want to think about.

Kiri's mom is only a little taller than Kiri. She's round and soft and laughing. Kiri's mom works at the bakery and brings home loaves of bread that we slice with the big serrated knife and eat with lots of butter. Kiri's mom is good at growing houseplants and giving cuttings from them to neighbors on the block. Kiri's mom takes Junie For Short on walks every morning because Kiri sleeps as late as possible. Kiri's mom planted the white pine for Kiri in their front yard when Kiri was born, like my parents planted the river birch for me.

Kiri's mom, Kiri's mom, Kiri's mom.

Lalala

Sometimes, these days, I have nightmares.

Not nightmare*s*, exactly.

One nightmare. *A* nightmare.

Over and over, the same thing: A darkening sky. Wind. Storm clouds. Lightning.

And . . . a *roar*.

Every time I have the nightmare, I claw my way out of it. Wake up sweaty. Panting. Heart racing.

Once I realize it's the nightmare—again—I lie in bed and watch the branches of my birch, outlined against the sky through my window. If I go downstairs and onto the porch and look down the block, I'll see Kiri's house, and Kiri's white pine in front, the same age as my river birch.

So I don't.

At first, in the weeks after Kiri left, I would wake up and for a minute, everything was normal. Ordinary. I'd lie in bed, stretch, yawn. Think about what Kiri and I might want to do after school.

Then I'd remember: Kiri was still away.

Sometimes, like now, I would hear Junie For Short down the block. Barking. Howling.

That's when I started the *lalala*. So I wouldn't have to hear Junie For Short, missing Kiri as much as me.

That's also when I went all around our house looking for Kiri things. I brought them all up into my room and put them in a wooden box.

I'm keeping them all safe for Kiri. I'm watching over them.

Things like the little glass with the puppy on it that I gave them for their fifth birthday. Kiri loved that glass so much they always brought it with them to my house when we had sleepovers.

The friendship bracelets we made for each other the summer we learned to ride bikes.

The tie-dye T-shirts we made in Kiri's backyard that one day.

The trick birthday candles I bought for Kiri's eleventh birthday. You know the kind that spark and fizz and won't go out no matter how hard you blow on them? That kind.

And the tree pictures Kiri and I made in Mr. Nesbitt's class that day, the day of dreaming big, of thinking way into the future.

Kiri turns eleven in three weeks, at the end of August. Trick candles are our birthday tradition. Trick candles and one non-trick candle to stick in the side of the cake.

The non-trick candle is the one to grow on. We keep the same candle and reuse it every year, on both our birthday cakes.

We call it our lucky candle.

I haven't told anyone, but I know Kiri will be home in time for their birthday. I'm sure of it. It'll be just me and Kiri and our parents and a big beautiful cake from the bakery where Kiri's mom works.

That big beautiful cake will have eleven trick candles on top, and the one little lucky candle to grow on, poking out of the side.

It'll be a birthday like all our other birthdays, with our parents laughing together and me and Kiri eating as much cake and ice cream as we want.

One of us will save our lucky one-to-grow-on candle, the way we always do, to use at my birthday next spring.

I'm counting on Kiri's birthday. I'm counting on our lucky candle. I'm counting on everything being back to normal by then.

This is how I go to sleep every night now: my door open just a tiny bit, my Kiri things safe in their box under my bed, thinking about how much fun it's going to be once Kiri is home.

Not thinking about the nightmare.

If I don't think about it, maybe it will go away and never come back.

Don't think don't think don't think

Don't think is another form of *lalala*.

It's hard not to think, and it's hard to *lalala*, but that's what you have to do if you don't want to think about your best friend being so far away.

Most of the time it works.

I sleep hard and deep and I don't have the nightmare and I wake up to the sun shining through the branches of my birch and like always it takes me a minute to remember that Kiri isn't just down the block like they've been all my life until now.

That's when I peek over the side of the bed to make sure the box of Kiri things is safe beneath it.

That's when I think *Twenty more days until Kiri turns eleven.*

Twenty more days until things are back to normal.

With enough *lalala* and *don't think don't think don't think,* I can make it until then.

I go downstairs and outside. And that's when I see something I've never seen before.

A telephone.

In my birch tree.

Nestled into the crook of the two limbs closest to the sidewalk, glinting in the sun.

What the heck is that?

I stand on the porch staring at it—is it a mirage? Are my eyes playing tricks on me?

That's *my* tree in *my* yard at *my* house and there's never been a telephone there before.

Push open the porch door. One-two-three-four-five down the steps. My bare feet know the way through the flowers to my tree—

It's not a mirage.

My eyes aren't playing tricks.

A telephone is perched in the branches of my birch tree.

Not just any telephone either.

This telephone is old.

Heavy.

Solid.

The kind of telephone your grandparents might have used. The kind with a base and a receiver and a circle to drag around for each number. The kind of telephone connected with a cord attached to the wall of your house.

But it's not connected to anything.

It's just sitting in my tree, in the crook of the limbs closest to the sidewalk, as if it's always been there.

Just then Mrs. S walks out of her house across the street, looks both ways, and marches over to me.

At the exact same time, Junie For Short starts barking, way down at Kiri's house.

I close my eyes and push myself against the trunk of my birch. I wish I could disappear right into it. I don't want to talk to Mrs. S. Or anyone. I just want the days to go by until Kiri gets home.

Too late. Everyone knows where to find me.

"Ayla?"

I open my eyes to see Mrs. S point at the old telephone.

"Where'd that come from?" she says.

I shrug.

"It didn't just appear on its own, did it?"

Again I shrug. Down the block, Junie For Short is still barking. This distracts Mrs. S from the telephone.

"You know what?" she says. "I think that dog misses you."

"I think that dog misses *Kiri*," I say.

I sound mean. I don't like the sound of my voice. But if Mrs. S is about to tell me I should go visit Junie For Short, she needs to know that no way am I.

Mrs. S looks down at me. I'm sitting in the special spot where two of the trunks are close enough for me to lean back against. It's my favorite place, just like Kiri has a favorite place in their white pine too.

Kiri and I have a secret code. When we're in our trees, we wiggle a certain branch.

If we see the branch wiggle, we know we're both home and both in our trees. But these days only one of us is home, so . . . no wiggling.

No looking down the block toward Kiri's tree either, just in case I forget they're not home and imagine I see the branch wiggle.

I don't want to get my hopes up.

I'm waiting for Kiri's birthday.

Back to the telephone, which is now in Mrs. S's hands.

"But where in the world did it *come* from?" she says.

Just then Pops comes down the front steps. Mrs. S holds the telephone up to him, frowning.

"Who knows?" I say. "Maybe it's magic."

Maybe it's magic.

I mean that as a joke, but the minute the words are out of my mouth they feel . . . real. It's a good thing Mrs. S is so focused on the telephone that only Pops hears me. Anyone else would laugh. Except maybe Gentleman. Gentleman's still little enough to believe in magic.

Pops doesn't laugh, though.

"You know what, Ayla?" he says. "You might be right."

Why is it in my tree, though?

"Maybe it's there just in case you want to call some-one," Pops says, as if he can hear my thoughts.

Well. That just sounds . . . dumb. Who can you call on a stupid old telephone not connected to anything?

Dumb and *stupid* are both words Martina used to say, back in second grade, and Kiri and I try never to use them.

But here I am, thinking them anyway. I keep my mouth shut so I don't actually say them.

"*Call* someone?" Mrs. S says in a warning kind of way. "Oh, Linden."

She hands the telephone over to Pops and walks back to her house, shaking her head. Still holding the telephone, Pops eases down onto the ground and stretches his legs out. Pops is kind of old.

When you look at his oak tree—the burr oak that his parents planted when he was born—you get a sense of how old he is, because Pops's oak tree is tall. Wide. Sturdy.

If it were cut down and you could count all the rings of all the years of the burr oak's life, it would take you a long time.

Pops hands the telephone to me and I take it. I don't want to, but I also don't want to be rude.

The telephone is heavy in my hands. It feels . . . important, somehow.

This telephone is way older than me and Kiri. Way older than my mom and dad. Maybe even older than Pops?

"Think about it, Ayla," Pops says. "All the people who've talked through this old telephone."

"What if I don't *want* to think about it?"

My voice has that tone again, as if I'm someone else, maybe the mean version of me. The Martina-from-second-grade version of me. But Pops just pats my shoulder, pushes himself up, and leaves.

You were rude to Pops, I think.

I don't want to be rude to Pops, but I was.

I don't want to look at Kiri's house, but sometimes I sneak a look down the block anyway.

I don't want to look at this telephone, this heavy, heavy telephone, but here it is, sitting on my lap.

Back in the day, you couldn't just pull a phone out of your pocket and go for a walk, or clear the dishes, or fold laundry, or water the trees on your block while you talked.

Nobody could.

Everyone had to pick up the receiver of a heavy telephone like this and dial a number and be connected to someone else's telephone with actual wires.

This old telephone is kind of like a tree.

Trees have to stay connected to where they're planted too. Trees push down into the ground, anchored by their roots. Tree roots talk to each other, in a way, underground.

If one tree's thirsty, other trees funnel water to it.

If one tree's hungry and in danger of starving, other trees funnel sugar to it.

If a tree is under attack from insects, it will send out a warning, and other trees make medicine to repel the bugs.

Kiri and I know all these things because we study trees. If you want to *be* a tree, you have to learn about trees.

I set the old telephone back in the crook of the two low birch limbs, right next to the sidewalk.

Just in case you want to call anyone, Pops said.

Both Pops and I have the feeling the telephone is magic, somehow. But how? Important, somehow. But why?

Maybe I don't want to know. I didn't ask for this telephone to appear in my tree and make me think about these questions.

I'm trying *not* to think. I'm trying to get through the days until Kiri comes home. Until we have their eleventh birthday party. Until cake and ice cream and trick candles and our one, lucky, candle.

Not long now.

The telephone just sits there, calm and still, as if it belongs in my tree, which annoys me. As if it's waiting for someone to pick it up and make a call.

Well, it's not going to be me.

Have you ever leaned back against the trunk of a tree for a long, long time, until it begins to *thrum*?

If so, you know how to turn part-tree. That *thrum* means the tree has accepted you. It's willing to be a home for you. The tree understands you won't try to hurt it—

won't carve your name into its trunk

won't pull off its bark

won't suddenly just . . .

go away

I'm mad at Kiri for going away, even if it's not their fault.

It doesn't feel right to be sad and mad at the same time. I lean back against my birch and wait for the *thrum*.

While I wait, I wonder where Kiri is, like right now at this very minute. I wonder if Kiri, right now at this very minute, is wondering where I am.

Which makes no sense, because Kiri *knows* where I am. I mean, I'm the one sitting in my tree. I'm the one not looking down the block at Kiri's tree and Kiri's house. I'm the one trying not to listen to Junie For Short howling.

I'm the one keeping watch over Kiri's things so that when Kiri comes back everything, everything, everything will be exactly the same.

"Ayla?"

Gentleman's voice. Argh! Why won't anyone leave me alone? But like I said, Gentleman is five. No one should be mean to a little kid.

"Hi Gentleman."

He points at the telephone.

"Did that grow there?"

If Kiri were here we wouldn't be able to look at each other, we'd be trying so hard not to laugh.

"Trees grow leaves," I say. "And branches and roots and seeds. But they don't grow telephones."

Gentleman nods. Just keeps standing there.

"What's it doing in your tree?" he says, after a while.

"I don't know. It just appeared."

"There has to be a *reason*."

"I guess so people can use it," I say, so he'll stop talking. "If they want to, I mean."

"To call someone?"

I nod.

"Who?"

"Whoever they want!" I say, louder than I meant to. Gentleman's used to his yelling parents, though, so he doesn't even blink. Which makes me feel bad.

"Can I call Sweetheart, then?" he says.

Oh geez.

"Gentleman," I say. "Sweetheart's *dead*. Right?"

"Yeah."

"So," I say, "you can't—"

call a dead lizard on a telephone in a tree, is what I'm about to say. But I don't finish the sentence. Because again, Gentleman's just a little kid.

"This is a magic telephone," he declares. "You can use this telephone to call anyone you want. But only if they're not alive anymore."

I stare at him. Where did *that* come from?

Then I think, maybe from the same place that *This is a magic telephone* came from.

First me and Pops, now Gentleman.

"If I can call anyone I want," Gentleman says, "then that means I can call Sweetheart!"

I don't point out that Sweetheart isn't an anyone, she's a lizard, because again, he's just a little kid. And also, what do I know about this telephone?

Nothing.

Behind me, in our house, Pops is whistling "You Are My Sunshine." That means he's making coffee. It might mean he's also making pancakes. If I smell melting butter, that means he's definitely making pancakes.

I sniff. Sniff again.

Definitely.

I'd rather think about Pops's pancakes than the strange appearance of a telephone that might possibly be magic. Also, I happen to know that Gentleman loves pancakes.

"You want some pancakes, Gentleman?"

"Before I call Sweetheart?"

It's not going to do you any good to call your lizard, I almost say. Along with *That telephone's not connected to anything, and besides, lizards don't talk on telephones.*

But I think of what Pops said, about *just in case you want to call someone,* and I stop myself.

"Sure," I say. "Pancakes before telephone calls."

Pops is making not just regular pancakes but corn pancakes. His specialty.

Gentleman and I sit at the kitchen table and watch him slice off long rows of corn kernels from ears he holds steady with one hand.

Pops adds the corn to the pancake batter and scoops spoonfuls into the sizzling butter.

"How're things, Gentleman?" Pops inquires.

"Not very good. Sweetheart died."

"Your gecko? I'm very sorry to hear that, little man."

Gentleman nods. "I'm going to call her after these pancakes. On the telephone of the tree. Because it's magic. And you can call anyone you want on it."

Pops just nods, as if that makes sense.

Which it doesn't.

"He's going to call his *lizard* on the *telephone*," I say to Pops, hoping he'll pick up on the weirdness.

But Pops just keeps making pancakes.

I beam my thoughts to Pops: *He thinks he can actually talk to his lizard on that telephone.*

But Pops just turns around and slides corn pancakes onto two plates, one for me and one for Gentleman.

"Sounds like a good plan," he says to Gentleman.

Gentleman's mouth is too full of corn pancakes to answer.

"Kiri was always a fan of my corn pancakes too," Pops says.

"*Is,*" I correct him. "You'll have to make more as soon as they get home."

"Are you going to call Kiri on the telephone, Ayla?" Gentleman says.

"No!"

I stop myself from saying a whole bunch more, like *How dumb* and *Why would I do that?* and *Don't talk about Kiri as if they're the same as your stupid lizard.*

Dumb. Stupid. I feel so bad even thinking those words. Gentleman is just this tiny little kid whose lizard died. It's not until Pops puts his arms around me that I realize I'm crying.

"It's okay to cry, Ayla," Gentleman says. "That's what Sweetheart used to tell me."

I feel even worse now. Poor little kid, thinking his lizard used to talk to him. But Gentleman jumps up and runs out of the kitchen.

"I'm gonna go talk to Sweetheart now!" he calls back.

"Pops!" I say when he's gone. "His lizard is *dead!* That telephone isn't *connected* to anything!"

Pops wipes his hands on the dish towel. It's as if he doesn't even hear me.

I give up and sneak out on the porch, and then onto the front steps, and then right up to my tree, so I can observe Gentleman.

Observe is the word Kiri and I use for what others might call *spying*.

Gentleman glances up at me, receiver in his hand.

"Ayla, help. I don't know what Sweetheart's number is," he says. "I don't know what number to dial."

Oh crud. That look on his face again. Those eyes, asking me for help.

Right then and there, I decide to lie.

"Any number will work," I say, just making it up. "All numbers will go straight to Sweetheart as long as you're the one calling."

"Really?"

"Yup."

He sticks his pointer finger in the dial and begins turning.

Kiri doesn't have a telephone where they are, so I haven't talked to them since the day they left. No post office, either, so I can't even send snail mail.

For one second, I feel jealous of Gentleman.

Gentleman twines his index finger in the telephone's twirly cord. He looks like a miniature old man.

"Hey," he says. "You there, Sweetheart?"

And that's how the telephone of the tree begins.

You hungry?

Gentleman's voice is a whisper.

Remember that time we locked the door on them and wouldn't open it?

They're still yelling, you know.

And once, so low I can barely hear him:

Sometimes I get so scared.

Finally, Gentleman hangs up. He stands there for a minute with his hand on the old telephone. Then he turns, looks straight at me, and gives me a peace sign.

Yup, a peace sign.

His little five-year-old swaggering self is back.

That old telephone glints at me from its crook in the tree. I stare back at it. Why did it have to appear in *my* tree? Why not someone else's tree?

I'm not about to make a call on it.

But something tells me I shouldn't move it, either.

So I lean back and

lalala

lalala

lalala

lalala my way right out of my thoughts and into my tree instead.

quiet myself—

breathe slow and deep—

look up at the leaves fluttering in the breeze, my tree and its leaves, my tree and its leaves, my tree and its leaves, until—

thrum

thrum

thrum

"Ayla?"

"Hey Ayla?"

Argh! More voices!

It's Geneva and Rowan.

The two kids who live in the duplex down the block. They've lived there since they were babies. Weeping willow Geneva and Rowan.

"Do you want to . . . walk to middle school with us?"

"When it starts, we mean."

Rowan and Geneva. Best friends whose parents are also best friends.

Geneva and Rowan, who run up and down the stairs and in and out of each other's apartments without asking, without thinking, just like Kiri and I run in and out of each other's houses—

"Well, Ayla? Do you?"

Stop it! *Go away!*

That's what I'm thinking.

The problem is that it comes right out of my mouth.

"Stop it! Go away!"

They stare at me, then look at each other.

"Whoa," Geneva says. "We were just asking if you wanted to walk to school with us."

"Yeah," Rowan says. "I mean . . . geez."

"It's *middle school,*" Geneva adds.

Like I don't know that? They peer in at me through the leaves and limbs of my tree. What am I, some kind of animal in the zoo? I hate the zoo. I hate people staring at me. I hate Geneva and Rowan.

Even though I don't *really* hate Geneva and Rowan. I'm just jealous of them. They have each other. Neither has to deal with the other being far away.

"Thank you," I say. "But I'll wait for Kiri to get home."

Again they just . . . look at me.

"Well," Geneva says after a minute. "Um . . ."

"Let us know if you change your mind," Rowan says.

The telephone glints at me again, so calm in the crook of my tree. I will it to go away, but it just stays there.

I lean back against the trunk of my tree, but the *thrum* is gone.

Help me.

Please help me, tree.

But just then a car goes up the street in the wrong direction and Mrs. S comes tearing out of her house, waving her arms and shrieking.

"WRONG WAY!"

Our block is a one-way street. Everyone drives in the same direction, everyone parks in the same direction. But sometimes a car hurries the wrong way up our one-way street and Mrs. S yells and yells and yells.

"WRONG WAY!"

"WRONG WAY!"

"WRONG WAY!"

The car just keeps zipping along, going the wrong way. Mrs. S used to get angry and shake her fist at wrong-way cars, but things got even worse when Kiri went away.

Now Mrs. S just keeps yelling until the car is out of sight. These days she's always on the lookout.

Always, always look both ways when you cross the street, all the grown-ups say. *Better safe than sorry.*

They've been saying this since we were tiny.

And we do look both ways.

Almost always.

Almost.

The almost always thing, the Kiri still not back home yet thing, the Geneva and Rowan walk to middle school thing, the Gentleman and Sweetheart thing, the telephone appearing in my tree thing.

None of it is what I want to think about, but the *lalala* and the *don't think don't think don't think* are getting harder and harder.

So is sleeping.

I keep having the nightmare. Over and over: wind, storm clouds, lightning, and that *roar*.

Sleep is easy when Kiri's around. Even when we have a sleepover and stay up late talking and laughing and whispering so Mom and Dad and Pops won't hear us.

I like to wake up when Kiri's sleeping over.

I listen to their soft breath.

I watch them and wonder if they're dreaming.

It's peaceful to be the only one awake on the block, and to know that Pops and my parents are just down the hall, and everything is quiet, and everything is safe, and everything will always be that way.

My hair is a mess.

My mom hasn't braided it in a long time. Not because she doesn't want to. Not because she hasn't tried.

But because I won't let her.

Braiding is a me and Kiri thing, something we do together. My mom sits one of us down in front of her knees, and then she sits the other one down, and we lean back against her knees while her fingers fly.

We love the feel of my mom's fingers in our hair, the twist and pull. We love how she makes different braids each time and never asks us what we want because we know that whatever she does will look good.

Every day my hair is more matted. More twisted. It'll be hard, when the day comes, to fix it.

I don't care.

Except I do.

I do care.

I want my hair back the way it's always been. I want my mom's fingers threading through it, so fast and sure and soothing, Kiri next to me waiting their turn.

But I also don't want my hair braided. I can't. I won't.

Not until Kiri comes home.

Don't can't won'ts are like *lalalas*. They stay down deep inside us, hidden like birds with folded wings—

folded wings that wait

and wait

and wait to

o p e n

but don't.

There are other *don't can't won't* questions in my head. Things that have to do with Kiri going so far away.

Kiri, Kiri, Kiri.

Kiri, Kiri, Kiri

sings itself in my mind

like a cry

When Kiri comes home it'll be the biggest relief in the world. Seventeen more days until Kiri turns eleven. Seventeen more days until cake and ice cream and eleven trick candles and one half-melted lucky candle to grow on.

In the meantime,

lalala lalala lalala

don't think don't think don't think

I'm scared of the nightmare.

Maybe I'll stay up all night.

If I stay up all night, it'll be only sixteen days until Kiri's birthday. I turn on the light and pull the wooden box of Kiri things out from under my bed.

I arrange them around me on my bed and send Kiri my thoughts.

Mostly my thoughts are one thought:

Come home.

Come home, Kiri.

Please come home.

On nights like this I look out the window at my birch tree, its branches outlined against the sky. My birch tree is always there.

My birch tree listens to all my silent questions and all my silent thoughts and all my silent wonderings, all of which are

LOUD

from all the silence

and all the

lalala

and

don't can't won't

buried inside

I must have fallen asleep, because when Dad knocks on my door, the sky is beginning to lighten and my lamp is still on. I quick cover all my Kiri things with my blanket before he sees them.

"How's my girl?" he says, sitting on the floor beside my bed.

"Okay. I guess. It was hard to sleep."

"Do you miss Kiri?"

"I just want them to get home."

"Yeah. We all wish Kiri could come home."

Those soft brown eyes. Those tough brown hands, hard from work, that are only soft when he strokes my cheek or smooths my hair back or holds my hand.

"Maybe you're nervous about school starting," he says. "Seeing as it's middle school."

I shake my head.

"Maybe it'll feel weird, being there without Kiri?"

I keep shaking my head. "Kiri'll be home by then. Only sixteen days now."

Dad gives me a puzzled look—*sixteen days?*—but I don't say anything else. He can't have forgotten Kiri's birthday, can he?

Outside my window, across the street, over Mrs. S's house and Gentleman's apartment building and Rowan and Geneva's duplex and the whole neighborhood and the whole city and the whole country, the sky lightens some more.

Streaks of pink and orange and red. Dad holds out his hand.

"Want to watch the sun rise?"

I like to sit in my tree at dawn and look out at our block, just beginning to wake up.

Dad knows that about me. So do Mom and Pops, but Dad gets up earlier than they do.

We both like to watch the block wake up.

Sounds of windows opening, a car rumbling to life, somebody with headphones on a morning run, feet *thump thump thumping* on the sidewalk, somebody else curving down the street on a bike, singing.

I like to watch the Spruce Café's neon *Open* sign blink on and know that Mrs. S will soon emerge from her house to pick up her daily blueberry muffin. Once in a while she gets pumpkin raisin instead.

Sunrise is when I used to watch Kiri's mom wander down the sidewalk with Junie For Short on a leash, so that Junie For Short could pee.

Sometimes Kiri's mom was still wearing her pajamas.

Sometimes I'd wiggle my birch limb at her even though she doesn't know the secret code.

I'm not doing any of those things now. I'm waiting until Kiri comes home and everything's back to normal.

The air is cool. It doesn't feel much like summer. School starts next month.

Middle school.

A new school.

But Kiri and I will be fine. We'll have each other, like always.

We'll walk to our new school together. No need for Geneva and Rowan. We'll walk home together. We'll sit in our trees. We'll take care of the trees on the block. Everything will be back to normal.

Dad and I sit on the front steps and look up at the glimmering sky, just beginning to spread its light over us all, and for one second I forget that Kiri isn't home yet.

For that second, looking out over our block, everything feels the same as it always has.

Everything I love is here, I think.

Everything I want is here.

Everything is possible here.

The feeling inside me is so big, it feels as if I might float away. Float higher than my tree. Float right up into that high bright sky.

If Kiri were home they'd just look at me and nod. Best friends can communicate without words.

Like trees.

Trees know when one is in trouble, and they all reach out to help the in-trouble tree.

Animals too, maybe.

Like when Junie For Short barks and barks down the block, the huskies—who live in the blue duplex with the violinist—sometimes howl too.

Trees and animals know how each other feels, and I guess people do too.

I mean, I knew Gentleman was sad even before he told me about Sweetheart.

Some of the people on our block reached out to me, when Kiri went away.

Like Mrs. S, who crossed the street a few days later, and came right up to me in my tree, where I was huddled up against the trunk.

"I'm sorry, Ayla," she said. "I'm very sorry that Kiri—"

"Had to go away," I interrupted.

Mrs. S looked hard at me.

Later I heard her tell Pops that he should keep a close eye on me. That she was worried about me.

"Ayla will do things in her own time," Pops said. "She'll be okay, Hazel."

That night I thought about the baby bunny Mom and I found once in the front yard, hiding in the phlox. It didn't move. It didn't look at us. Was it hurt? We were worried.

Mom picked it up to see what the matter was, and the bunny didn't move once, not until she put it down again.

The whole time Mom was holding it, the bunny didn't act scared at all.

The bunny acted as though everything was fine, as though being picked out of the flowers where it was hiding and held in the hand of a giant human was perfectly natural.

We didn't know that bunnies make their nests on the ground. We didn't know we should leave it alone.

But even so, I knew the bunny was terrified on the inside.

I could feel it.

When something huge happens inside our hearts and minds, humans sometimes turn still and silent like that bunny.

Like me, the day Kiri went away.

Now Dad puts his arm around me and nods in the direction of Kiri's house. I don't want to look, but . . .

I do.

Early sun filters over Kiri's white pine. I look at the special branch, but it's still, as still as the whole tree.

Then I see it.

Something new.

A baby tree, so tiny, in Kiri's yard opposite their white pine.

A baby *birch*. A birch tree, like *my* birch tree.

I jerk my head around and look at Dad. His brown eyes are steady, as if he's waiting for me to say something.

But instead of saying anything, I push him. Hard. I slam my hand down onto his leg.

"What!" I yell. "Is that! Doing there!"

I've never hated a tree before but I instantly, completely hate that tree. Mean words like *ugly* fill my mind.

That little ugly baby new tree.

Just one more reason not to look down the block at Kiri's house, and Kiri's white pine, and Kiri's dog, and that new

ugly

baby

tree

wilting

away

in

the

sun

and

lalala

Dad doesn't tell me to stop yelling. He doesn't tell me not to push and slap. He doesn't ask me why the sight of that tiny baby new tree in front of Kiri's house upsets me so much.

What Dad does is put both arms around me and rock me until I stop the *lalala*.

Then he tells me Mom had to go to work early, and to wake Pops and let him make me breakfast. And off Dad goes to the big city lot, to climb up into his garbage truck and start his rounds.

I don't wake Pops.

I lean back in my tree instead.

I imagine Kiri next to me, leaning back against my tree.

We're planning our day.

Maybe we'll float down the creek on our blow-up rafts.

Maybe we'll go to Arbor Ice Cream. I picture Kiri with a rhubarb sorbet cone like always, and me with peanut butter swirl like always.

Maybe Pops will take us to Sycamore Park by the river so we can stand on the shore and tilt our heads up, up, up to see the crowns of the sycamores, the oldest and biggest sycamores for hundreds of miles.

Imagining that Kiri's home and we're planning out our day is soothing. It's familiar. It's the way it's always been: me and Kiri, Kiri and me.

And it's also a little bit like *lalala*

Like *don't think don't think don't think*

Like *don't can't won't*

There's one problem, though.

Correction: There are *two* problems.

One problem is the old telephone, sitting silent in the crook of my tree, waiting for someone to make a call.

The other problem is that little baby tree wilting in the sun all the way down the block at Kiri's house.

Even if I never look down the block at that tiny tree again, I still know it's there.

I can tell it's thirsty. It could use a big bucket of water, trickling slowly into the ground all around it, soaking into its roots, helping it grow tall and strong.

Someone else can haul a bucket of water to that baby tree if they want to. It's not going to be me.

There are only two reasons a baby tree gets planted on our block. The first is because a new baby was born. And the other is because . . .

I never met my grandmother. She passed on before I was born, and Pops planted our butternut tree in her honor. Off to her grave he goes every Sunday, with flowers and trowel and all the week's stories to tell his Randa, who according to Pops

is always waiting

to hear them

"It's beautiful, isn't it?" Kiri always says, when Pops talks about Randa. "It's so beautiful, how much he still loves her. How he still just . . . talks to her."

But where is she now?

Is my grandmother in a different world?

Is she somewhere else in this same world only—

invisible?

What my parents and Pops say about *passing on,* how
it happens to everyone—

    is something I

    don't want to think about

    don't want to imagine

    when it's soooo far away still

    and by then

    Kiri and me will be old and gray

    walking with canes

    and hearing aids

    in a faraway time

    a faraway place

    a lifetime of me and Kiri

    between now and then

The sun is fully risen and the day fully begun. Dad at work, Mom at work, Pops making coffee in the kitchen.

There's Mrs. S, walking back from the Spruce Café with her muffin.

There's the violinist, taking her huskies out for their morning run.

There's Junie For Short at the end of a leash, coming down the block toward—

not me

I freeze. Push back against my tree, willing Kiri's mom not to cross the street, not to look at me, not to say anything to me, not to—

Oh.

Wait.

It's not Kiri's mom at the other end of the leash.

It's Geneva and Rowan. What are *they* doing, taking Junie For Short for a walk?

Geneva and Rowan don't even *know* Junie For Short! They don't even know Kiri's mom! They don't even know where Junie For Short likes to go on her walks!

Kiri and I are the ones who know. Kiri and I are the ones who take Junie For Short on her walks. What. The. Heck.

They better not come near me. They better not stop at my tree.

And they don't.

They don't even notice when Junie For Short turns her head to stare at me from across the street. She stares and stares and stares until they drag her on past.

Lalala

Don't think don't think don't think

My eyes are closed. I press hard against the trunk of my birch. I stay there a long time, pressing and not thinking about that baby tree. Not thinking about Rowan and Geneva and Junie For Short, how she stared at me.

"Hello?"

I open my eyes. A boy is peering through the leaves at me. Not a boy, a man. A boy-man on a Galaxy Pizza delivery bike. No one I know. Maybe he's in high school or college and this is his summer job.

"Do you live here?" he says. "Is this your telephone?"

He's still on the bike, one foot touching down to keep it steady, helmet shading his face.

"Not really," I say. "It's the telephone of the tree."

I don't tell him it's *my* tree. That's obvious, I guess.

Pizza Delivery Bike Guy keeps looking at me, like there's something he wants to ask me.

But I already know what he wants. I can sense it. Once again, words just come out of me.

"It's a magic telephone," I say. "You can call anyone you want on it."

That's all it takes.

Bike Guy hops off his bike and picks up the receiver.

His voice isn't loud, but it carries anyway.

"Dad," he says.

Pause.

"Dad," he says again. "I keep thinking about that day . . ."

Pause.

"Look. I know you were pissed at me." His voice gets quiet. Almost a whisper. "But here's the thing. We would've talked. We would've worked it out. Like always. Right?"

Pause.

"Can I tell you something? Dad. I miss you. Okay? Like, I really, really miss you."

His voice is different now, in a way I recognize. Bike Guy is trying not to cry.

It doesn't seem right to look at Bike Guy when I know he's crying, or close to crying.

But it also doesn't seem right to just . . . ignore him.

He sets the receiver back down on the telephone and swipes at his eyes. He doesn't put his helmet back on. He doesn't go back to his delivery bike either. He just stands there on the sidewalk in front of me and my tree.

If I were a tree, fully a tree, what would I do? I would sense what was troubling Bike Guy, and I would try to help him.

So I think of the words he said and the way he said them. I try to think my way into Bike Guy's heart.

But guess what? I don't have to.

I already know how Bike Guy feels.

He'd had a fight with his dad. They were angry. They would've worked it out, like always.

But they didn't, and now Bike Guy is stuck here, without his dad, missing him.

And the only way he can talk to him is on the telephone of the tree, just like the only way Gentleman can talk to Sweetheart is on the telephone of the tree, because Sweetheart and Bike Guy's dad are . . .

... passed on.

When I think of Bike Guy and his dad, there's only one feeling in my own heart.

Sadness.

"I called my dad," Bike Guy says. "He can't, he's—"

His voice chokes up again and he doesn't finish.

What can I do?

How can I help?

A small curl of birch bark lies on the ground. I pick it up and give it to him. A gift from my tree, my tree and me. Something he can hold.

That night I can't fall asleep.

Again.

This time it's because I keep thinking about Bike Guy. And Gentleman. And their calls on the telephone of the tree.

I pull the wooden box with Kiri's things out from under my bed.

"Hi," I say to each one in turn.

The little glass with the puppy on it.

The friendship bracelets.

The tie-dye T-shirts.

The trick birthday candles.

The half-melted one-to-grow-on candle.

The tree pictures we made that day in Mr. Nesbitt's class.

I arrange them in a semicircle around me on my bed and look at each in turn.

Mom and Dad are already asleep in their room down the hall. They have to get up early for work.

Downstairs, in the kitchen, Mrs. S and Pops are talking. Both were born on our block and grew up on our block and still live in the same houses. They went to elementary and middle and high school together.

They've been friends their whole lives, like Kiri and me.

The burr oak and mulberry trees their parents planted for them are tall and strong.

I think about those tall, strong, big trees. They started out as babies, like all of us. They're exactly as old as Pops and Mrs. S. Sometimes I wonder if the trees are friends too.

I always picture Kiri and me someday being like Pops and Mrs. S, who still visit each other and drink Pops's coffee and eat Mrs. S's cookies.

Eleven more days until Kiri's birthday.

How many birthday candles are there?

Enough for when Kiri turns eleven?

I'm pretty sure there are eleven. Plus the half-melted lucky candle, the one to grow on.

I decide to count, just to be safe.

Just in case there aren't quite enough.

Over and over I count: one two three four five six seven eight nine ten eleven. Slower now.

One

Two

Three

Four

Five

Six

Seven

Eight

Nine

Ten

Eleven—

Pops and Mrs. S always call each other by their real names, Linden and Hazel.

Pops: Slow. Soft-voiced. "Hard to believe it's already been this long, isn't it, Hazel?"

Mrs. S: Quick. Not soft-voiced. Full of opinions. Full of *Young man, where is the adult supervision?* when it comes to Gentleman, and *Young lady, tell that grandfather of yours I could use some corn pancakes* for me, and *It's not always easy to use "they" instead of "he" or "she," but child, I promise you I am trying my best* for Kiri.

"Linden, I'm still so angry at that driver," Mrs. S says. "If he had just been paying attention. Just seen he was on a one-way . . ."

Her voice floats up the stairs from the kitchen and into my room, like wind.

Angry at the driver?

I look at my Kiri things, spread out around me on my bed. Kiri and I like to spy on Mrs. S and Pops. It's funny to hear them laugh about people they knew back in high school and the things they did. Kiri likes to hear them call each other by their real names, Linden and Hazel.

It's weird to think that Linden and Hazel were once our age.

I scoot closer to the door, the better to hear.

"I don't get angry at the driver, no," Pops says. "Sad, maybe. I get sad, Hazel."

"It's so unfair to the child," Mrs. S says.

The second I hear Mrs. S say "the child" I know who she's talking about. Even though Pops and Mrs. S are downstairs and they have no idea I'm listening, I tense up, as if they're both looking at me.

The child is me. I can feel it.

"Linden, has she talked about it yet?"

Pops doesn't say anything for a while.

"She'll talk in her own time, Hazel."

"But don't you *worry,* Linden?"

"Of course I worry."

"And you're just going to let her be? Let her just sit in that tree, not talking, not . . . doing anything?"

"Don't assume she's not doing anything, Hazel."

"But I see her there, day in and day out. I overhear things. Did you know that Geneva and Rowan came by the other day and asked her to walk to school with them when it starts?"

"I did not."

"You know what she told them? To stop it. To go away. That she was waiting for Kiri to come home."

"Well," Pops says, "then maybe we should listen."

Mrs. S makes a *tsss* sound. That means she's exasperated.

"Linden."

"Hazel."

"So you're really just going to let your granddaughter sit in that tree the rest of her life? Is this the way you and her parents intend to handle what happened?"

"We handle things in different ways, Hazel. What about you? Every time a car goes by in the wrong direction, you come screaming out of your house."

"That's because I'm watching over the children on the block, Linden! I watch all the cars so what happened that day never—"

Mrs. S breaks off talking.

I close my eyes. I don't want to think about cars speeding the wrong way up our one-way street either.

"You're as worried as the rest of us," Mrs. S says after a little while.

"Ayla will deal with the situation when she's ready to."

Mrs. S has known Pops all his life. Longer than I have. So she must hear the steel in his voice. In his quiet way, Pops is telling her to *be quiet*.

"In the meantime, you've seen the telephone in Ayla's tree, Hazel," Pops says. "Feel free to use it anytime. Call anyone you want on it."

Mrs. S snorts. *As if,* her snort says.

I look down at the old oak planks of my room, scratched but still shiny. There's a long pause from the kitchen. Maybe they're done with their not-quite-argument. Maybe Mrs. S will get up now, and walk across the street to her own house. I wish she would.

But she has one more thing to say.

"You know who would hate this situation more than anybody?" Mrs. S says. "You know who'd hate knowing that Ayla is just fading away like this?"

I quick close my ears up and *lalala* so I won't hear Mrs. S's voice anymore. I know whose name she's about to say and I don't want to hear it.

But I hear it anyway . . .

Kiri

My hands fly out and gather up all Kiri's things and shove them underneath the blanket so Kiri can't see or hear.

Even though Kiri isn't here.

Lalala

Don't think don't think don't think

When I open up my ears again, Mrs. S has left. The only sounds are Pops, moving about the kitchen, clinking dishes and running water.

Next morning, Gentleman tells me it's good that the telephone never leaves my tree.

"Just in case someone needs to make a call in the middle of the night," he says.

Again I roll my eyes inwardly. Who would ever make a call on that telephone in the middle of the night?

No one, I think.

But turns out Gentleman is right.

Because late that night, I'm kneeling by my window, watching people passing on the sidewalk. A car door shuts. A lone, late skateboarder cruises down the middle of the street.

And just then, someone steals up to the telephone of the tree.

Who is it?

I stay still and silent, crouched on the floor, and peer down at . . .

Mrs. S.

She stands in darkness next to the telephone, outlined by the faint glow of the streetlight. She looks small in the shadows.

Mrs. S reaches toward the telephone, cradled in the crook of the limbs, then drops her hand back by her side. I watch her shoulders rise up in a tiny shrug and then fall.

Then Mrs. S trudges back across the street and disappears into her dark house.

Who did Mrs. S want to call?

I think about how Pops told her she could call anyone on the telephone, anytime she wants. I think about how Pops once told me how much she had loved her husband, Douglas.

I think about how Pops talks to my grandmother Randa all the time.

"You can always talk to the people you love, baby girl, whether they're here or not," Pops says.

Mrs. S doesn't, though. I've never, ever heard her talk about Douglas.

I think about how Gentleman asked me if the telephone grew out of my tree. Maybe it wasn't such a silly question.

Trees talk to other trees, even ones far away, through their connecting root systems.

People talk to people who aren't right next to them through telephones.

Maybe the telephone of the tree is a gift of the tree, to the humans who need it.

Because everyone who's made a call on my telephone, the telephone of the tree, has called someone . . . passed on.

Gentleman called Sweetheart.

Bike Guy called his dad.

Mrs. S *wants* to talk to someone on it, even if she hasn't . . . yet.

While I'm being patient, and waiting for Kiri to come home, I notice everything Kiri's missing:

the buzz of cicadas

butterflies floating from blossom to blossom

bees bumbling at the phlox and coneflowers

birds hip-checking each other at the bird feeder

I store them up to tell Kiri when they finally come home.

Come home, Kiri

Kiri, come home

I feel myself reaching out to Kiri, the way tree roots reach underground. Is Kiri reaching out to me too?

The telephone watches and waits.

When I go to bed I tell Dad how to turn part-tree. How the *thrum* is a sign.

"Trees talk to each other, you know," I say.

Then I tell him how Gentleman talks to Sweetheart on the telephone of the tree. I tell him about Bike Guy. I even tell him I saw Mrs. S sneak up to the telephone late last night.

The lamp in my room is low and soft. My birch whispers its limbs against the screen.

Soft breeze.

Soft night.

Soft feel of Dad's palm, smoothing my hair back, smoothing and smoothing.

But inside my head the *lalala* is waiting.

"Dad?" I say. "It's only a week until Kiri's birthday and Kiri's still not home. And Kiri *has* to be home for their birthday party."

Dad gives me a funny look.

"Birthday party?" he says.

"DUH!" I say, loud. Because how can he forget Kiri's birthday? How can he forget we *always* celebrate it? "Kiri's going to be *eleven*!"

The branches of my birch tap-tap-tap against my window.

"It takes a while, daughter," he says. "Takes a while to get used to something, doesn't it?"

"There's nothing to get used to!" I say. "I just want Kiri to get home!"

"I know you do, daughter."

"Can I show you something?" I say, and I reach down for the hidden wooden box under my bed.

I open the box and let him look through it.

He picks up the friendship bracelets and the tie-dye T-shirts and the trick birthday candles and the puppy glass. He holds the half-melted one-to-grow-on candle and turns it over in his palm, smiling in a sad kind of way.

One by one, he studies all my Kiri things.

Finally, he picks up our tree pictures from the *What Do You Want to Be?* day in Mr. Nesbitt's second-grade class. The dream big day.

Those he holds gently in the palms of his hands and studies. Tilts his head a little.

He doesn't say *What are these* or *Did you make these friendship bracelets* or *So that's where the trick candles went.*

Dad doesn't say anything at all.

He just puts everything back into the wooden box. The tree pictures come last. He puts them on top of the other things in the box.

Closes the lid.

Puts the box back beneath my bed.

"You know what those are, daughter?" Dad says. "Talismans. Kiri's things are talismans. Special things to keep you safe."

"Special things to keep *Kiri* safe," I say. "To keep safe for Kiri, until they're home."

"Maybe both," Dad says.

Both.

Wherever Kiri is now, in that place where I can't text and can't call and can't write, I can keep their things safe for them.

Dad pulls the blanket over me and tucks me in.

"Sleep tight, my tree girl," he says.

That night, the nightmare doesn't come.

Maybe it's Kiri's things, keeping me safe.

I dream instead of the telephone in the tree. How it just appeared. In my dream the telephone *thrums,* just like the trees do, just like Kiri and I do when we turn part-tree.

In the morning I wake up and count.

Six days until Kiri's birthday, and Kiri's still not back.

Mom and Dad are at work when I come downstairs.

"That little birch in front of Kiri's house isn't doing too good, Ayla," Pops says. "You noticed that?"

I never look down the block at Kiri's house, so how could I notice it?

"Looks as if it could use some water," Pops says.

"I didn't plant that tree," I say. "It's not my problem to take care of it."

Pops nods, like maybe he expects me to say that.

"Kiri's mom shouldn't have planted that stupid tree," I say. "Kiri already *has* a tree."

Pops looks up at me—we're not supposed to say *stupid* or other mean words in our house—but he still doesn't say anything.

Maybe he can tell how bad I feel, having just called a tree stupid. I mean, a *tree*.

I sound like Martina from second grade.

That afternoon, Bike Guy returns on the Galaxy Pizza delivery bike.

"I come back here sometimes now," he says. "When I need to talk to my dad."

He nods toward the telephone. Then he reaches into the pocket of his shorts and pulls out the little curl of river birch, the tiny piece of my tree I gave him.

"I keep this with me," he says. "Thank you."

"Thank my tree," I say, but not in a mean way.

Bike Guy stands there looking at me. His eyes are searching.

"Listen," he says. "Did something like . . . me and my dad happen to you too?"

I start to shake my head but . . .

I'm so tired

so tired

of always shaking my head

of always not talking

of all the

lalala

and the

don't can't won't

that I look up at Bike Guy and just . . .

sigh.

He frowns. Not in a mean or angry way, but in an *I'm sorry* kind of way. An *I know what it feels like* kind of way.

"So there's someone you call too?" he says, glancing at the telephone.

But to that, I do shake my head. Fast and hard.

No.

Back in second grade, when Mr. Nesbitt told us to draw what we wanted to be when we grew up, he told us to be aware of both negative and positive space in our drawings. It was hard to understand what he was talking about, back then, but now I know what he meant.

Mr. Nesbitt said positive space is the thing you're drawing, and negative space is everything around and between it.

Negative space is invisible, the things you don't see.

But invisible is what makes everything around it full of color and shape and life.

Just like what you *don't* talk about is as important as what you do talk about.

Maybe more important.

I used to see only the positive space of Kiri, which is Kiri laughing and talking and running down the block toward me. Kiri wiggling the branch in their tree. Kiri and Junie For Short sprawled out on the living room floor, Kiri's head pillowed on Junie For Short's belly.

The day Kiri went away was the day I realized how much negative space there is in the world.

Kiri was everywhere.

And now, everywhere I look, Kiri isn't.

It's early evening, the time of day that Kiri's mom calls the golden hour, when the air gets still and the sun is nearly set, and I'm on the front steps watching the world turn shimmery.

A man comes down the sidewalk, a sleeping baby in a front-facing sling on his chest. He's walking the way parents of sleeping babies walk sometimes, hands holding their baby's feet, or supporting their little butts.

Then he stops by my tree.

"Hi there," he says. "Are you the keeper of the telephone?"

The keeper of the telephone.

Am I?

I shrug. And sigh, but he can't see that.

"A guy at Galaxy Pizza told me about you," the man says. "About your telephone, I mean."

Bike Guy, I think.

But I don't say anything. The baby wakes and looks at me, dark eyes sizing me up.

"Is it okay if I make a call?" the man says, tilting his head at the telephone.

Before I can nod, he picks up the receiver and angles it, as if he wants the baby to hear too. I start to roll my eyes inwardly but then I picture Bike Guy, and Gentleman, and Mrs. S, and I don't say anything.

"Lindsay?" the man says into the telephone.

He jiggles the baby, who looks up at him and smiles.

"It's me. Me and Siena."

The man takes a deep breath and puts one arm out to steady himself against my birch.

"Listen, Linds," he says. "I don't want you to worry. I figure you being you . . ."

He pauses and closes his eyes. The baby stares up at him.

"That maybe you *would* worry," he finishes.

The baby reaches up and pats his cheek.

"You want to say hi to your mama, Siena?" he says, and holds the heavy phone against the baby's tiny face.

The baby laughs and bats it away. He smiles and holds it against his own ear again.

"I talk to her all the time about you," he says. "She's happy, like you hoped she'd be. She had her first bite of pizza yesterday."

"Galaxy, of course," he says. "I told her how it was your favorite."

Baby Siena reaches out to the birch leaves closest to her. In the last of the golden hour light they glow against her skin.

"The pizza guy told me about this telephone. He said he comes here and talks to his dad, when he needs to."

Pause.

"Remember what I told you, Linds, right at the end? Not to worry, that I got this?"

His voice drops to a whisper, but I can still hear him.

"We miss you. But also, we're okay."

Three more days until Kiri's birthday.

I don't talk about the birthday party anymore. I don't want to see those weird looks on anyone's face. Anyway, Kiri will be home by then.

Kiri will be home by then.

Kiri will be home by then.

It's the happiest thought I have, and I say it over and over and over.

So why don't I feel happy?

Time to pull out the wooden box. Time to count up the candles, make sure there are enough. Time to gather my Kiri things around me so the nightmare won't come.

But it comes anyway—

shiver of lightning

crack of thunder

roar of wind

blare of—

then the sound of my own voice inside my own head—

KIRI!

KIRI!

KIRI!

I claw my way out of the nightmare, out of sleep, into the soft light of the lamp that Mom must have turned on, because there she is, sitting on my bed, rocking me back and forth.

"Another bad dream?"

Dad's voice, from the doorway, so soft, it's more of a whisper. Mom nods.

But the nightmare isn't just when I'm asleep anymore. It's inside me when I'm awake too. It gathers itself inside me like lightning, like thunder and rain and wild wind about to explode me.

I creep my fingers under the blanket, gathering Kiri's talismans, clenching them in both hands.

Dad comes to sit on my bed too, as Mom rocks me. He puts his hands over mine, over the blanket, over the talismans.

Downstairs there's the sound of the porch door closing with its little scrape. Pops must be up late again. Maybe he was sitting on the front steps the way he likes to do. Now there's the soft creak of his feet on the wooden floor.

I look out the window at the darkness.

No moon.

No light.

"I've been having trouble sleeping too, daughter," Dad says.

"Me too," Mom says.

I can tell they're waiting for me to say something. To ask why. Which would be polite.

But being polite is hard. It takes effort.

And I'm so tired.

Tired of talking to people, even my own people, like Mom and Dad and Pops. And Mrs. S. And Gentleman. And Geneva and Rowan. And Kiri's mom, even though I haven't talked to her at all. She's the one I most don't want to talk to.

I'm so tired of not talking

not crying

not screaming

Dad. Mom. Just leave me alone.

Leave me alone.

Leave me alone.

"Why can't you sleep?" I say, finally.

"Because our girl keeps having nightmares," Mom says.

Shhh. Shhhh. Shhhhhhhhhh.

That's the sound of me talking to myself inside my head. Telling myself to be quiet, be quiet, be quiet, not talk, not say anything, not say anything about my *nightmares,* which aren't even *nightmares,* they are just

one

single

nightmare

over

and

over

"Not night*mares,*" I say. "Night*mare.* Only one."

Now I'm angry at myself. For saying something. For saying anything.

I don't want to talk about my nightmare.

Don't want my parents, or Pops, or anyone, even to know about it.

I just want my nightmare to go away, and for Kiri to come back, and for the birthday party to happen three days from now, and for everything to be good and ordinary and regular again.

Kiri's talismans are warm in my hands. They like being under the blanket. They like that I'm holding them so tight. I hold them tighter and tighter and tighter. I'll never let them go. I'll keep watch over the talismans until Kiri—

pop

The tiniest pop in the world happens then, and Mom and Dad and I all hear it.

My right hand is suddenly wet. Something hurts.

oh no

oh no

oh no

oh no

I broke the puppy glass. Kiri's favorite glass. The glass I gave them on their fifth birthday because Kiri wanted a dog and their mom said no it was too much responsibility and no matter how much Kiri promised and promised and promised and promised that they'd take responsibility and they'd take such good care of the dog and never have to be reminded, Kiri's mom still said *No*.

Which was why I, who knew how much Kiri wanted a dog, got them that puppy glass.

The puppy glass was a reminder.

A reminder not to give up.

Not to lose hope.

Not to let the no-you-can't-have-a-dog get to you. Not to let the *no no no's* embed themselves in your heart. Not to let yourself get smaller and smaller and smaller. Not to let yourself stop dreaming, stop hoping, stop thinking that what you most want in the world will happen.

To think big, dream big, want big.

Be big, Kiri and I used to say to each other.

"STILL say to each other!" I hear myself say out loud. "Not *used* to say!"

My parents stare at me, confused.

I turn my head away.

Beneath the blanket my hand hurts. The hurt is getting worse. The lamplight is soft, it's late, everyone should be asleep but we aren't and now look at us, me and my mom and dad and Kiri's broken puppy glass and a hand that hurts

worse

worse

worse

here on our block of trees and dreams and wishes and hopes and

lalala

and

don't can't won't

Kiri, do you understand that I'm keeping your things safe and I'm waiting for you to get home and I count the birthday candles to make sure there are enough and

Kiri Kiri Kiri

I'm still hoping

still dreaming big

and I will never

ever

ever

give up

Dad pulls the blanket down and there in the late-night lamplight of my late-night room are

broken shards of puppy glass

trickles of blood falling from my hand

"Ah, baby girl," Mom says, and Dad joins in, "Ayla, Ayla."

Their voices are the softest sounds in the world, soft like the breeze when it sighs through the leaves of my birch, my birch, my birch, my birch.

Mom holds my bleeding hand in hers and turns it this way and that, her eyes searching.

"It'll be okay," she says finally. "It's a single straight cut. Not deep. We were lucky."

We.

Not "you."

We're lucky.

Are we lucky?

Dad gets a towel from the bathroom and wraps it around my cut hand.

"Stay right here," he says, as if I would be going anywhere.

He brings back a wet washcloth and some ointment and gauze. Mom cleans and bandages and wraps my hand. By the time she's done it doesn't hurt as much.

They sit back down on the edge of my bed and Dad smooths my hair back from my forehead. It feels good. It feels Dad-like, the way Mom braiding my hair feels Mom-like. It's been so long since Mom braided my hair.

"So. You want to tell us about this nightmare?"

If I tell them about my nightmare, I'll have to go back to that day, the day Kiri went away.

That awful day.

"No," I say. "Not yet."

But when, then?

When?

Everything in me, lungs and heart and stomach, clenches up when I think about that day, that day I don't ever want to think about.

But not thinking about it means that it's all I *am* thinking about.

Trying to push it away means I can't ever get away.

Not letting myself live through it means that I just keep living through it.

Is that why the nightmare keeps coming? Because I keep pushing it away?

That day.

That day.

Kiri and me had made our plans. We were going to take Junie For Short to the creek so we could all wade along the edge and look for minnows and peepers.

It was spring.

The creek was running fast. The air was full of possibility. This would be our first visit of the year to the creek with Junie For Short.

The air was also weird, though.

The kind of weird it sometimes gets in warm weather, which that day was. Oddly warm, for spring.

Kiri and I looked up at the sky. It was the kind of blue-gray it looks in spring sometimes. But the air, the air was changing.

"You think it's going to storm?" Kiri said.

"Yeah."

But so what? We could go to the creek, right? We could just take cover under a tree, along the bank, if a storm came.

Not if it was a lightning storm, of course. But if it was a rainstorm, that'd be okay. We would just get wet.

All these thoughts raced around my mind and Kiri's. We didn't have to talk out loud because we knew what the other was thinking.

"Be big!" Kiri said, and "Dream big!" I said, and Kiri jumped up and ran down the block to get Junie For Short.

If we walked fast, jog-walked, we could get to the creek before it rained.

But the block itself seemed still.

So still.

Too still.

Thunder clouds hung heavy and low. The wind whooshed to life, bringing fury and wildness with it. Lightning shivered across the dark clouds. Thunder boomed.

Dang it.

No way could we go to the creek in this kind of weather. Plus, Junie For Short is terrified of thunder. When Kiri and Junie For Short got to my house we could just stay on the porch and watch the storm.

Storm watching is something Kiri and I like to do.

I sat on the front step and waited. Where were they? It was taking a long time.

Thunder boomed behind flickering clouds.

The air was heavy.

The trees of the block were hushed and watchful, waiting for the storm to crash down.

Gentleman was nowhere to be seen. My parents and Pops were inside.

The violinist in the blue duplex was practicing her violin, a wild up and down song that felt like an echo to the wind and thunder. Her huskies sang along to the music in their unearthly way.

Someone zipped down the street on an electric scooter, but I didn't even look up.

Mrs. S was in her front yard across the street, darting looks at me. Then she was on the sidewalk, arms crossed, frowning.

"Go inside, child," she called. "This is dangerous weather!"

I didn't move. I ignored the wild wind.

"I'm just waiting for Kiri and Junie For Short!" I yelled across the street at Mrs. S. "Then we'll go inside!"

But the wind and thunder were too loud for her to understand what I was saying.

Down the block at Kiri's house, all the branches of Kiri's pine bowed and waved in the wind. Mrs. S made shooing motions with her arms now, trying to shoo me back into my house.

"I'm just going to run down there and see what the hold-up is," I called to Mrs. S, who still couldn't hear me.

I should have been careful.

But I wasn't careful.

And neither was Kiri.

I ignored the thunder, which rumbled and cracked and boomed and took up all the space for sound in the air. I ignored the lightning. I ignored the air now turning green and ominous, and I ran down the steps to the sidewalk.

No one called to me when I ran down the steps. Or if they did, I didn't hear them.

Other things were happening. Tornado sirens, wailing across the city.

The huskies in the violinist's window, muzzles pointed to the sky, wailing along with the sirens instead of the music.

Mrs. S still out front on her sidewalk, staring up at the sky and then at someone—

KIRI

at the end of the block sprinting down their front steps—down the sidewalk—

toward me—

calling Junie For Short—

Junie For Short! Come back! Come back!

Because Junie For Short, who was terrified of thunder, had somehow escaped her leash and was racing down the middle of the street—

Mrs. S yelled and yelled.

Get back in your house this minute, Kiri! RIGHT NOW RIGHT THIS MINUTE THAT'S A TORNADO SIREN—

but her words blurred together.

Kiri ran after Junie For Short, who ran toward me while sirens wailed and huskies howled and Mrs. S yelled and somewhere a door banged and a car engine revved and the sky above began to pour down water and a **roar** started up and the **ROAR** grew louder but Kiri and I just wanted to get Junie For Short safe to my house just get her safe get her safe—

Junie For Short tore across the street to me and leaped onto me wild-eyed and terrified and behind her was Kiri—

Kiri, who didn't look both ways

Kiri, who didn't look even one way

What Kiri did was jump

one foot off the curb

into the street

splashing in the rain now pouring down

while Kiri's mom came leaping down the steps of their house, shouting

Kiri!

Kiri!

Kiri!

. . . and the sirens wailed and the huskies howled and Mrs. S screamed and Junie For Short struggled wild in my arms and the car horn blared and the **ROAR** got louder and that was when I realized that the blaring car and the **ROAR** were the same thing—

not a tornado siren, not a tornado,

but a car

a car racing the wrong way down our street toward

Kiri

Kiri

Kiri

and that was when

Kiri

Kiri

Kiri

went away

It happened so fast. It happened so fast. It happened

so fast

    so

    so

    fast

    that my mind had to

    catch up

    to what was

    happening

    to what had

    to what had

to what

had

already

happened

When something huge happens, time slows.

Or maybe it stops, just for a little while.

Just for a minute, maybe.

Like the day I slipped on the ice and fell flat on my back by the garage. I didn't know what had happened because it happened so fast.

One second, I was running to the truck because Dad and I were going to a movie, and the next I was looking up at something white and huge—the huge white sky—and the back of my body was suddenly cold.

Everything felt the same, but different.

A second later I understood that I was lying on my back looking up at the sky, and my mind click-click-clicked backward:

sky

ice

fall

slip

The day Kiri went away was like that.

Time slowed down.

Or maybe it stopped, just for a moment, while it was happening, while Mrs. S was shouting and Kiri's mom was running and Junie For Short was wild with fear and the sirens and the huskies and the screeching of the car's brakes and the no the no the no the *nooooooo*

Because that second of time, the second when time stopped, was

long enough to remember—

long enough to live through memories—

long enough to go backward in time—

to all the sleepovers

all the dinners

all the everythings

Kiri's puppy glass
friendship bracelets

tie-dye T-shirts

trick birthday candles

old half-melted candle to grow on

tree pictures

softness of Kiri's breath when they were asleep in my
room at night

softness of their braids

how they crinkled their nose when they drank something cold

the all of it

came rushing through me

on the day

Kiri

went

away

And

all my *lalala*

all my *don't think don't think*

all my *don't can't won't*

since that day

haven't really worked

I burrow into my parents' arms and arrow my thoughts

to Kiri, my you-and-me our-whole-lives-long Kiri—

babies reaching our hands to each other

babies laughing at each other

babies lighting up

at the sight

of each other

Kiri and me

and all our plans

for the future

until I finally
fall
asleep

When I wake up, it's morning and my parents are gone. My bandaged hand hurts, but not too bad.

Kiri's talismans are lined up on the windowsill, shining in the sunlight, my birch branches outside the window watching over them.

Creak of Pops's feet on the kitchen floor.

Faint smell of maple syrup and melted butter and pancakes, stronger as I head downstairs.

Pops puts a big plate in front of me, along with the jug of maple syrup. He squeezes my shoulders and doesn't say anything, just watches me eat.

When I walk out to my tree the telephone is waiting. Nestled in the crook of the limbs. Glimmering.

Despite myself I look down the block at that baby birch tree. The baby tree that never would've been planted if Kiri hadn't gone away. The baby tree that will always remind me of the storm, with its

lightning

thunder

wildness

and the car that came racing the wrong way, the wrong way, the wrong way

There will always be the flashing red and blue lights of the police car

There will always be the ambulance siren

There will always be the huskies howling and howling and howling

It's then that I finally pick up the receiver.

Because I can't do this by myself anymore.

"It's always going to be there, Kiri," I whisper into the telephone. "That day and everything that happened is always going to be in me."

I close my eyes and wait. The telephone *thrums* in my hand. My birch leaves flutter in the wind.

That day will always be there

but there's more, Ayla

so much more

The sun streams down and the sky is purple-blue and all the trees on our block, our block of beautiful, beautiful trees, are lit up as if every one of them is telling me there's more, there will always be

so, so much more

When I hang up, I wrap my arms around my birch tree. Lay my cheek against its rough papery bark.

I think about Kiri's house. Kiri's mom. Junie For Short.

It's hard.

More than hard.

It's been a long, long time.

A long time since Kiri's mom sliced open a big loaf of still-warm bread from the bakery and we spread slices thick with butter and handed them around the table and tore off tiny pieces from our slices and gave them to Junie For Short.

A long time since we all sat there laughing and eating and laughing and eating.

A long time since Junie For Short pushed her cold nose into my leg because she wanted to go for a walk.

I'm not the girl I used to be.

I'm not the girl they used to know.

I'm not the girl I was even in that last minute, when Kiri ran down the block after Junie For Short in the wild wind and wild rain and wild thunder—

Breathe. Breathe.

Up and down the block, all the trees glow and shine.
All the beautiful trees, talking to each other and to me.

Begin again, Ayla. Don't get stuck now.

I close my eyes and go back to the day Kiri went
away—

Say it, Ayla.

The day Kiri went—

went—

went—

the day Kiri—

died

Kiri's voice is inside me, still talking to me.

That day will always be there

but there's more, Ayla

so much more

Is there so much more?

Remember our tree pictures, Ayla.

That day in Mr. Nesbitt's class. The rough paper. The crayons. Martina with her frown. Kiri and me with our white pine and our birch and all the negative space that I didn't think about back then but I do now.

The beautiful negative space surrounding us.

I stand on the sidewalk and peer down at the end of
the block

at

that

little

baby

tree

That day will always be there
but there's more, Ayla
so much more

Behind me, in our house, Pops sits at the kitchen table drinking his coffee.

Mrs. S is in her house, in her kitchen—I can see her through the front window, moving around—probably making coffee too, the way every grown-up I know does.

Every grown-up except Kiri's mom, anyway. Kiri's mom makes tea in the morning: cinnamon tea with sugar and milk that she stirs and stirs and stirs while she sits dreaming at the kitchen table.

Today is the day.

Kiri's birthday.

Oh, Kiri.

I don't let myself think. Instead, I walk down our steps and down the block to the stop sign—

I look both ways and cross the street

for the first time

since that day

I turn my eyes away from the baby birch.

I focus on Kiri's steps. Kiri's door. The two welcome mats turned in opposite directions because Kiri's mom says that way when you leave the house the world welcomes you, and when you come home, the house welcomes you.

So no matter what, you're always welcomed.

I look at the mats, I look at the door.

I look at the everything of Kiri's house.

It's early.

If Kiri were here, they'd still be asleep, even though it's their birthday.

If Kiri were here, I'd push open the door without knocking, walk on in because I'm welcome, I'm always always welcome, and sit down by Kiri's mom at the kitchen table.

Watch her stir and stir and stir her tea while she dreams herself awake.

Should I?

Could I?

Ayla. It's time.

I reach up to push the door open but—

I don't have to—

because while I'm reaching, the door is opening and

there she is

Kiri's mom

and a big blur of fur
wiggling and pushing and making that
high
whine
that Kiri and I
always call
the love song of Junie For Short

It's almost too hard to look at them.

Their faces are too familiar.

Too loved.

Too missed.

How long has it been?

Too long.

Junie For Short pushes her cold nose into my hand. She wiggles and shakes against me. She sings and sings and sings her love song.

I wait while Kiri's mom looks at me, and then . . .

    small streams begin to move inside me

    first a trickle

    then a steady flow

    of sadness

    sorrow

    grief

    longing

    and also

    hope?

    there's more, Ayla
    so much more

Kiri's mom pulls me inside and hugs me all the way into the kitchen, where she bends down so she's my height, and she wraps me up in her arms, and we're like my birch tree with its separate but connected trunks.

Junie For Short pushes her way between us, and all three of us just stay there

there in the kitchen

there where Kiri and I grew up

there where Kiri isn't anymore

but

still, somehow

is

because this is where Kiri lived

and breathed

and sang and laughed and danced

The negative space *is as important as the positive space,* Mr. Nesbitt told us. *Always remember that.*

I breathe in the scent of Kiri's mom and Kiri's house and Junie For Short's fur and somehow, layered underneath it all, Kiri. All of it, all of it.

fresh baked bread

rosemary and basil and mint

sunshine and dust

old wooden table

soapsuds

all the smells of Kiri's house

all the smells of Kiri

We sit at the table, the old wooden table, there in Kiri's kitchen on Kiri's birthday with the flowered curtains waving in the breeze through the window screens, and the electric teakettle humming as the water inside comes to a boil

just like always.

There are the orange mugs and the cinnamon-spice teabags, and Junie For Short's muzzle resting on my leg, her eyes gazing up at me, her tail a metronome

back and forth

back and forth

back and forth

After a while of being in Kiri's kitchen it's still hard

and

it's also

a little easier

Kiri's mom pours boiling water into the orange mugs and dips the teabags in and out of the hot water.

She brings milk and sugar to the table and spoons sugar into her mug and a little milk.

The last time Kiri's mom and Kiri and I all sat together at their table was the morning of the day it happened.

Last times come for everyone.

That's something I know now that I didn't know then, in the spring, the last morning all of us were together at Kiri's house.

Kiri's mom passes me the sugar and milk and I add some to my mug of tea, just the way I've watched her do a thousand times.

"I've never seen you drink tea," Kiri's mom says, "but somehow I thought you might want some today."

The first words either of us have said since I walked into the house.

"It's my first time," I say.

First times come for everyone too.

My first time drinking tea, my first time being in the house since Kiri passed on, my first time being without Kiri on their birthday, my first time saying anything to their mom since that day.

"Some days I wake up and everything feels normal," Kiri's mom says. "And then . . . I remember."

"Me too," I say.

"Do you remember what today is?" their mom says, and I nod. I think of the trick candles and the half-melted one. Talismans now, all of them.

Junie For Short whimpers and pushes her nose into each of our legs in turn, and I feel her dog sadness, and her dog confusion, as if the same thing happens to her every morning too.

Then Kiri's mom says something that surprises me.

"You know the telephone in your tree?" Kiri's mom says. "Sometimes I call Kiri on it."

I've never seen Kiri's mom use the telephone of the tree. I haven't once seen Kiri's mom by my house since the day it happened.

"Only in the middle of the night," she adds. "I didn't want to upset you. You've been so, so sad. Junie For Short and I have felt it, all the way down here at the end of the block."

I nod. I think of all the times I didn't let myself look down the block. All the times I heard Junie For Short howling, and drowned out the sound with the *lalala*.

"How do you think it works, Ayla?" she says.

I don't know. But then again, maybe I *do* know, because the *thrum* of the telephone is the *thrum* of my tree.

"Maybe it's like trees," I say. "Trees know when another tree is hurting. Trees try to help."

Kiri's mom smiles. "Well, you and Kiri always did want to be trees."

I wonder what Kiri and their mom talk about on the telephone. But I don't have to wonder, because Kiri's mom tells me, as if she heard me thinking.

"We don't talk about much," she says. "What I'm doing. What I had for dinner. If the bakery had a special that day. Where I walked Junie For Short. How much I miss them. And how . . ."

Kiri's mom hesitates. "How *you're* doing," she finally says. "But . . . I haven't known what to say."

"Not too good," I say.

Which is the truth.

I look out the window at Kiri's white pine, planted when Kiri was born. On the other side of the little lawn I can just make out the top of the tiny birch tree.

Kiri's mom follows my eyes.

"Did you plant that in honor of Kiri?" I say, and she nods.

I think for a while. Mrs. S planted a ginkgo in honor of her husband, Horace, because he loved ginkgo leaves. Pops planted a butternut in honor of my grandmother Randa because she loved butternuts.

But Kiri loved pine trees.

"Why a birch tree, though?" I say.

"Because birches are your favorite tree," their mom says. "And you were Kiri's favorite person."

I can't look at Kiri's mom just then, so it's good that Junie For Short is pushing her cold nose into my arm. She keeps looking up at me, willing me to look at her.

I bend down so Junie For Short and I are on the same level, put both hands on the sides of her head, and look into her eyes.

She makes the sound she used to make when Kiri and I were in my tree.

Hmm-mm-mmm?

Hmm-mm-mmm?

This is Junie For Short's way of talking human.

I know exactly what *Hmm-mm-mmm?* means too.

"Come on, Junie For Short," I say.

I hook up her leash and we head out the door. I don't look at Kiri's mom and she doesn't look at me, which is good.

Kiri's mom understands. She understands that hearing the words *you were Kiri's favorite person* makes me want to cry and wail and howl like Junie For Short.

And it also makes me feel . . . loved. Loved the way only Kiri loved me.

There's so much more, Ayla.

This is the first time I've taken Junie For Short on a walk since Kiri . . .

since Kiri.

Maybe I'll think of it that way: since Kiri.

There was a last time that Kiri and I walked Junie For Short together, even if we didn't know it was the last time. And now there's a first time: Ayla and Junie For Short on a walk without Kiri.

"What do you think, Juniper?" I say.

Junie For Short tips her head and looks at me inquiringly.

Wait, what have I just called her?

Juniper?

Kiri and I never called her Juniper!

I stop, there on the block, right in front of Mrs. S's mulberry tree. The dog looks up at me. She's patient. She just waits.

"It's another of those things, isn't it, Junie?" I say.

We never called her just Junie either. Junie-For-Short-Juniper-Junie looks up at me and wags her tail slowly, as if she isn't sure she should be wagging it at all and she wants to do the right thing.

This is another one of the firsts.

Another first Kiri isn't here to laugh at or frown at or give me one of their *what the heck is* THAT *all about* looks.

"I wish Kiri was here, Junie-June," I say, and we plop down, then and there, by Mrs. S's mulberry tree.

Junie For Short.

Juniper.

Junie.

And now . . . Junie-June.

I just keep calling her names that Kiri and I never once called her. Junie For Short lays her head on my lap and looks up at me.

It comes to me that school will start, and I'll walk through those doors without my best friend. Into all those new classes without my best friend.

Wherever I go, the negative space of Kiri not being there will go too.

There's more, Ayla. So much more.

Next to me, Juniper thumps her tail as if she can hear Kiri too, and she agrees.

"We'll just keep going, won't we, June-June?" I say.

We'll just keep going together, through all the firsts to come.

"Hi Ayla," a voice says.

"Hi, Junie For Short," another voice says.

Geneva and Rowan, there on the sidewalk next to Mrs. S's mulberry tree, smiling at me and Juniper. Both of them a little uncertain. Junie softly thumps her tail, as if she too is a little uncertain.

"Hi Geneva," I say. "Hi Rowan."

"So . . ." Geneva says, then stops, as if she doesn't know what to say next.

Maybe as if she's a little scared of what to say next. Maybe even a little scared of . . . *me*?

I guess I can't blame her.

"If it's okay," I say, "can I walk to school with you both next week?"

Late one fall night Pops and I are sitting outside on the front steps, just the two of us, late at night, looking up at the harvest moon.

Round and yellow, it floats in the sky behind the branches of Pops's huge oak tree.

Baby Siena's dad came by earlier to make his weekly call. This time Siena was in a stroller, and he held the phone to her ear the way he always does.

When he left he called to me—"Bye Ayla!"—and Siena waved.

"Where do you think the telephone came from, Pops?" I say. "For real, I mean?"

Pops is quiet for a while.

"That telephone belonged to your grandmother and me," he says, finally. "When we were young."

"Pops! So it was *you* who put it there?"

He nods.

"And after Randa passed on, when I missed her especially bad," he says, "I got the idea to call her on it."

We sit there in silence for a while.

"Now I just talk to her whenever I want," he says. "I don't need the telephone anymore."

But you said it was magic, I almost say, and then I remember.

It was *me* who said it was magic, and Pops who agreed. And now I know the telephone really *is* magic. Just ask all the people who've used it.

Including me.

The telephone is part of the tree now, as if it grew there from the start.

Gentleman still talks to Sweetheart on it every day. He swaggers down the block and picks up the receiver, tells Sweetheart what he had for breakfast, what he ate for school lunch, what he wants for dinner.

Most of Gentleman's conversations are food-related, now that I think about it.

But also: Gentleman talks to Sweetheart about his parents. Whether they're yelling more, fighting more, or whether things are more peaceful.

Lately they seem more peaceful.

I keep an eye on Gentleman. He can be annoying, but also? I love him.

Kiri loved him too.

My tree and I watch over everyone: our neighbors, passersby, anyone who comes to our block to use the telephone:

Gentleman.

Kiri's mom.

Galaxy Pizza Bike Guy.

Baby Siena and her dad.

Mrs. S, who finally called Mr. S, and now checks in with him once a week or so.

Even Geneva, with Rowan by her side, once picked up the telephone. She wanted to talk to her grandfather, who died a couple of years ago.

She wanted to tell him something she didn't have time to tell him before he died.

That's what most people want.

Because none of us know when we'll run out of time.

Me? I don't need the telephone anymore. When I want to talk to Kiri, I just . . . talk. We were always good at knowing what each other was thinking.

We're still good at it. Maybe because long, long ago, we taught ourselves how to turn part-tree. And trees know how to talk to each other whenever they need to.

Down the block, Kiri's baby tree is growing.

It's growing taller fast, and its leaves aren't crinkled anymore.

That's because someone's watering it.

Someone's taking care of it.

Someone whose best friend's name was Kiri.

Trees have to take care of each other, you know?

Someday, a long time from now, all the trees on our block will be gone.

But for a while, the history in their rings will remain.

Kiri and I used to go search out stumps so we could count up all the years of the trees' lives. So we could study them and what they had lived through.

We saw which years were hard years: years of drought, years of fire, years of people carving their initials into their trunks.

We saw good years too. Easy years. Years when days and months flowed into each other, years of rain and sun and breeze and enough of everything.

Kiri and I watered the trees on our block when it didn't rain because that's what trees do for each other and we wanted to be trees.

Be big, Ayla.

I hear Kiri's voice sometimes, reminding me there's more. Reminding me to dream big, to be big.

Maybe someday I'll tell the story of me and Kiri to a little kid. Maybe a little kid on the block. Maybe a little kid who's *my* little kid.

In my mind that little kid looks kind of like Gentleman. They're full of questions like Gentleman too.

"So how did you meet Kiri?" the little kid will say.

"We met when we were babies," I'll say, and then I'll show them photos of baby Kiri and baby me by our baby trees. "Our parents planted trees when we were born."

And then I'll point to Kiri's pine and my birch. They'll probably be huge by then.

"What did you used to do way back then?" the little kid might say, as if I'm soooo old.

Which maybe to a little kid is the way I'll seem, the way thirty seemed soooo old to me and Kiri back in second grade, when we first drew our trees.

"We used to sit in our trees," I'll say. "We had a secret code."

I'll tell them about the pictures we made in Mr. Nesbitt's class. Maybe I'll show them the talismans I still keep in the wooden box.

Maybe I'll tell them how the puppy glass came to be glued together.

I'll for sure tell them about Pops and his pancakes with maple syrup, Kiri's mom and the fresh bakery bread with lots of butter.

The little kid might want some pancakes at that point, and I'll make them some.

With corn.

And butter.

And maple syrup.

I'll tell them about Pops, how I used to go with him to my grandmother's grave. How he would talk to her and I would listen.

"And where is Pops now?" the little kid might ask.

"Same place Kiri is," I'll say. "Same place my grandmother is. Invisible."

Invisible, and everywhere.

They're a shimmer in the wind, or a laughing bird, or falling leaves brushing our arms. Snow melting on our cheeks. A blanket when we're cold.

Maybe, even, a tree.

Author's Note

In 2016 I listened to "Really Long Distance," a story produced by Miki Meek on the NPR podcast *This American Life*, about a lonely telephone booth that stands in a hilltop garden outside the town of Otsuchi in northern Japan. In the telephone booth sits an old-fashioned disconnected rotary dial telephone that people from all over use to call deceased loved ones. The phone booth is the creation of Itaru Sasaki, who built it in the wake of his cousin's death in 2010. But when the 2011 earthquake and tsunami devastated Japan, others began coming to the phone to call their own loved ones.

From the moment I listened to this story, I was haunted by the phone booth and the people who come to whisper their questions and longings and love into the "phone of the wind," as it's known in Japan. The image of the phone and the reason for its existence was so powerful to me that I knew, right away, I wanted to create a book inspired by it. It took me many years before *Telephone of the Tree* finally felt right, and I am forever grateful to the beautiful act of grief and connection that inspired this novel.

Acknowledgments

My thanks to all those who helped in the long creation of this novel, including Itaru Sasaki, who in 2010 created the telephone that would become known as the "wind telephone" in his hilltop garden in northern Japan. To Aria Dominguez, first to lay eyes on *Telephone of the Tree* six years into the writing process, thank you for your instant love and support of this book. Dan-ah Kim, your beautiful art just makes me happy. To Sara Crowe, my huge thanks for finding the perfect editor. To Lauri Hornik, thank you for being that perfect editor. Your calm clarity and wisdom are invaluable. Birgitt Kollmann, magician translator, thank you for the heart, soul, and love you have brought to all my books. Finally, for all readers missing the voices of their loved ones, this book is for you.